This Book Belongs to:

RICHARD SCARRY'S
Great Big
Schoolhouse

STERLING and the distinctive Sterling logo are registered trademarks of Sterling Publishing Co., Inc.

Library of Congress Cataloging-in-Publication Data

Scarry, Richard.
  Richard Scarry's great big schoolhouse : abridged version / written and illustrated by Richard Scarry.
     p. cm.
  Summary: Follows Huckle Cat through a busy day at school, as he learns the alphabet, enjoys the playground, and participates in show and tell.
   ISBN-13: 978-1-4027-5820-1
  [1. Schools--Fiction. 2. Cats--Fiction. 3. Animals--Fiction.] I. Title. II. Title: Richard Scarry's great big school house. III. Title: Great big schoolhouse. IV. Title: Great big school house.
  PZ7.S327Rkfs 2008
  [Fic]
2007051046

Lot #
10   9   8
12/14

Published by Sterling Publishing Co., Inc.
387 Park Avenue South, New York, NY 10016
In association with JB Publishing, Inc.
41 River Terrace, New York, New York
On behalf of the Richard Scarry Corporation
This book was originally published in 1969 by Random House, Inc.
© 1969 Richard Scarry
Copyright renewed 1997 Richard Scarry 2nd
Copyright assigned to Richard Scarry Corporation

Distributed in Canada by Sterling Publishing
c/o Canadian Manda Group, 165 Dufferin Street
Toronto, Ontario, Canada M6K 3H6
Distributed in the United Kingdom by GMC Distribution Services
Castle Place, 166 High Street, Lewes, East Sussex, England BN7 1XU
Distributed in Australia by Capricorn Link (Australia) Pty. Ltd.
P.O. Box 704, Windsor, NSW 2756, Australia

Sterling ISBN 978-1-4027-5820-1

For information about custom editions, special sales, premium andcorporate purchases, please contact Sterling Special SalesDepartment at 800-805-5489 or specialsales@sterlingpublishing.com.

Designed by Elizabeth Azen

RICHARD SCARRY'S
Great Big
Schoolhouse

STERLING

New York / London

GETTING READY FOR SCHOOL

Huckle's mother woke him up.
"It is time to get up for school," she said.
"Why do I have to go to school?" asked Huckle.
"All children go to school to learn how
 to read and write," said his mother.
"You want to be able to read and write,
 don't you? Now please get up."
Huckle got up.
He yawned and rubbed the sleep out of his eyes.
He walked to the bathroom.

He washed his face with
soap and warm water.

He brushed his teeth.

He combed his hair
with cold water.

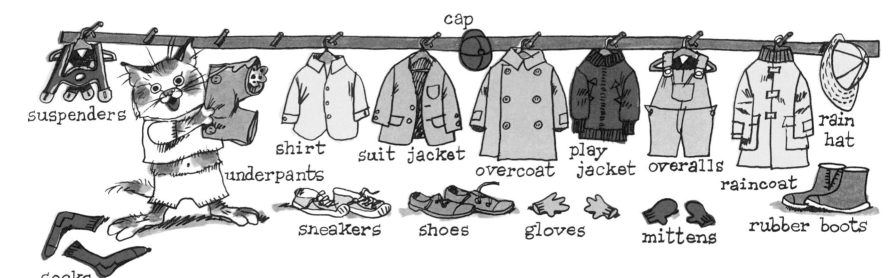

Then Huckle got dressed.
That is NOT the way to put on your pants, Huckle!

2

Mother Cat served hot cereal
to Huckle for his breakfast.

bowl
teapot
cup
saucer
spoon
brief case
fork
knife
tablecloth

Lowly Worm stopped by on his way to school.
"Hurry or you will be late for school," he said.

bacon
eggs
glass

"LATE! My goodness! I am late for work," said Father Cat.
He picked up his briefcase and ran.
Oh dear! He picked up the tablecloth, too!

Mother Cat walked with
Huckle to the school bus stop.
Honk! Honk! The school bus
came to take the children to school.

SCHOOL BUS STOP

SCHOOL BUS

RIDING ON THE SCHOOLBUS

black train locomotive

red and green coach

Every day Huckle rides to school in his orange school bus.
He sees many colorful things. Everything has a color.
What color is the fisherman's suit?

purple jeep

SCHOOL BUS

manhole

street

red motorcycle

Bananas Gorilla and
his yellow Banana-mobile

BUGDOZER

orange airplane

white ambulance
with red crosses

railroad crossing gate

crossing guard

traffic light

blue sign

red fire engine

yellow
crosswalk

GO
RIGHT

sidewalk

green taxi

fisherman

TAXI

tugboat

brown delivery van

bridge

river

THE SCHOOL

This is Huckle's school.
The school bus stopped in the schoolyard.
The school bell rang.
It was time for school to begin.
But what was all that noise outside?

weather vane

postman

bell

clock tower

CENTRAL SCHOOL

principal's office

schoolyard

6

policeman

chimney sweep

school
crossing
guard

School library

classroom

classroom

classroom

classroom

classroom

doctor's office

SCHOOL BUS

SCHOOL

Why, it was Joe, the janitor!
As usual he was late for school.

7

balloon

alphabet

Aa *Aa* Bb *Bb* Cc *Cc* Dd *Dd*

string

clock

bell

wall

notice board

calendar

teacher

SEPTEMBER

SUN	MON	TUES	WED	THU	FRI	SAT
		1	2	3	4	5
6	7	8	9	10	11	12
13	14	15	16	17	18	19
20	21	22	23	24	25	26
27	28	29	30			

map

umbrella

overshoes

desk

pupils

THE CLASSROOM

This is Huckle's classroom.
And behind the big desk sits Miss Honey, his teacher.
Every morning the pupils say, "Good morning, Miss Honey."
And every morning she says, "Good morning, children.
My, don't you look bright and fresh this morning!"
She always says that.

8

ceiling

Ee *Ee* Ff *Ff* Gg *Gg* Hh *Hh* Ii

overhead light

paper airplane

spider pupil

blackboard

window shade

window pane

spelling lesson

cat
dog
worm

arithmetic lesson

$$\begin{array}{r} 2 \\ + 2 \\ \hline 4 \end{array}$$

a pupil
who is late
for school

wastebasket

stool

window sill

Huckle's chair

table

Lowly Worm's chair

pencil sharpener

paste pot

paper clips

scissors

blackboard
eraser

ruler

eraser

Aa Aa
Bb Bb

chalk

Richard Scarry's
What Do
People Do
All Day?

storybook

pencil box

workbook

pencil

marker pen

thumb tacks

ball-point pen

push pins

9

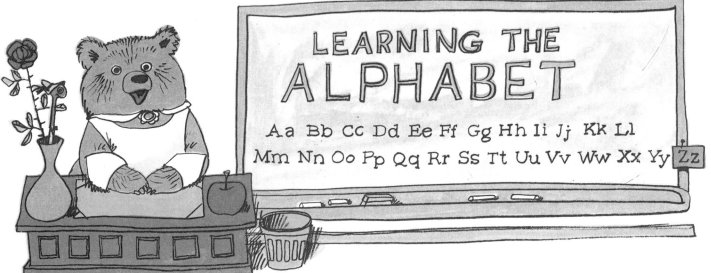

LEARNING THE ALPHABET

Aa Bb Cc Dd Ee Ff Gg Hh Ii Jj Kk Ll
Mm Nn Oo Pp Qq Rr Ss Tt Uu Vv Ww Xx Yy Zz

Each day Miss Honey teaches her class something new.
Today she was going to teach them the alphabet.
She gave each child a card with one of the letters
of the alphabet on it. Everyone tried to think of words
that began with the letters on the cards.

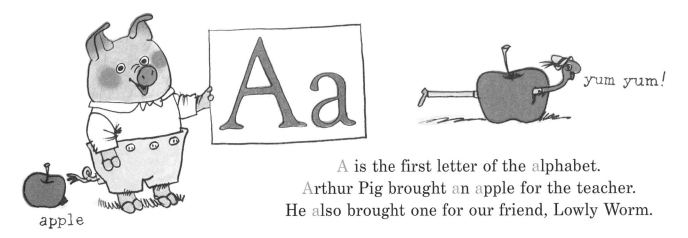

yum yum!

apple

A is the first letter of the alphabet.
Arthur Pig brought an apple for the teacher.
He also brought one for our friend, Lowly Worm.

broom

bowl

book

bench

"Bananas Gorilla! Take that Bananamobile
back outside where it belongs!" said Miss Honey.
"And please eat your breakfast at home!"

banana

10

Charles Anteater drew a car with his crayon.
He showed it to the class.

Donald Walrus danced up
and down on his desk.
Did you see the drawer pop out?

Elizabeth emptied her purse
and found some earrings.
She put them on.
They were extra heavy.

Frances Raccoon showed the children her doll furniture. Lowly Worm turned on the bathtub faucet and pretended to be a fountain.

Gloria Fox strung glass beads on a green string. She forgot that there are two ends to a piece of string. Bugdozer gathered up the runaway beads.

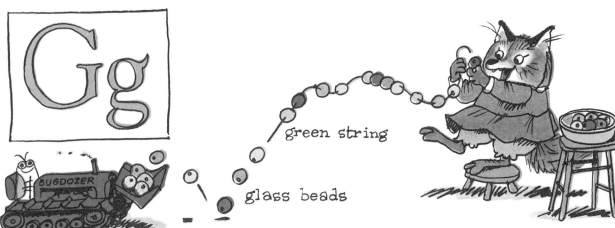

Huckle blew hard on his horn. Lowly was hiding inside it. Now Lowly knows how to fly!

Isabelle and Irving are eating ice cream. Irving, that isn't the ideal way to hold your ice cream cone!

Jimmy Crocodile spread orange juice
on his bread and poured jam in his glass.
Now just a minute! Isn't that wrong?

Kathy is wearing a kerchief. Lowly is shaking the ketchup. Kathy is showing
us things that are used in the kitchen. Never touch sharp kitchen knives.

All right, Lowly!
How many things can you name
that begin with the letter "L"?

Very good, Lowly!
Now, please take your seat.

ladder

lemon

log

lantern

loaf
of bread

leaf

lamp

letter to mail

lettuce

lunch box

laundry

Mildred Hippo is a magician.
She can make things disappear.
She put a melon in her mouth.
She munched on it.
It disappeared! Mmmm! Good!
My! What a marvelous trick!

Mm

melon

nut

nose (or trunk)

Nn

noggin

I am a nut
balancing
a card
on my noggin

napkin

new suit

Ned's turn was next.
He balanced a nut on his nose.
He wore a napkin because he did not
want to get any crumbs on his new suit.

Oliver Octopus has many
objects to show. He often forgets
to take off his overcoat in the
classroom. He played an old
lullaby on his oboe.

Oo

orange

oil

onion

oboe

oak
leaf

can-opener

oar

Peter Puppy put a sunflower plant
in his pocket. He pointed at it.

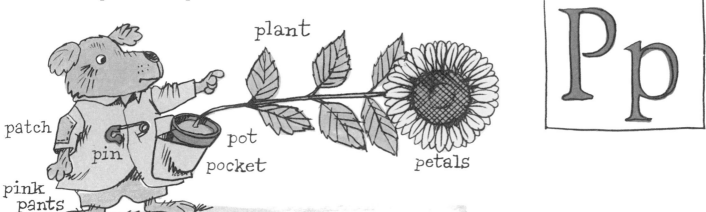

plant

petals

pot

pocket

patch

pin

pink
pants

P p

Please be quiet, children. Oswald Owl has a question to ask you.
"How many quarter pieces of pie are there in one whole pie?"
You are quite right! Each whole pie can be divided into four quarters.

Q q

whole pie

1
2
3

quarter
piece

4

Ruth Rabbit has a ribbon in her hair.
She has a rose in her left hand.
Huckle has a ribbon under his right foot.
Bugdozer is rolling up the rug.

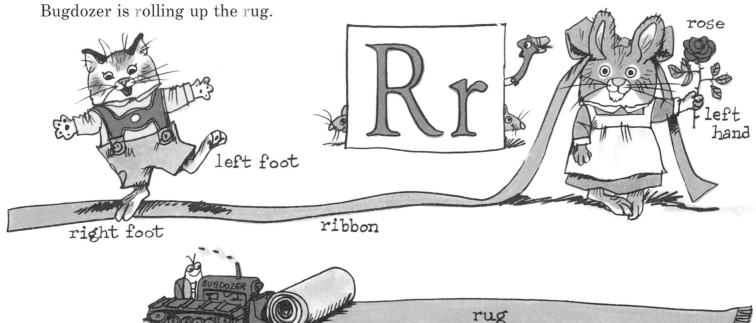

R r

rose

left
hand

left foot

right foot

ribbon

BUGDOZER

rug

15

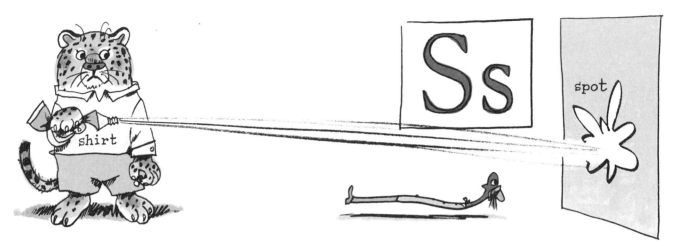

Spotty Leopard showed his schoolmates a tube of paste.
He squeezed it. It squirted. It made a spot. Paste is sticky.
Miss Honey told Spotty to get some soap and water.

Tom Tiger told everyone how to tie a knot.
He took two pieces of twine and tied them together.

Victor Bear showed some
pretty violets and a vine in a vase.
He tripped on the vine.

Ursula Pig stays
under her umbrella
when it rains.
She has used it a lot.

watch

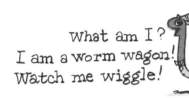

What am I?
I am a worm wagon!
Watch me wiggle!

wheel

Willy Fox can't think of one word that begins with a "W." Can you help him?

Lowly showed the class how he plays the xylophone with one foot.

Yvonne dropped an egg on the floor so everyone could see the yellow yolk inside.

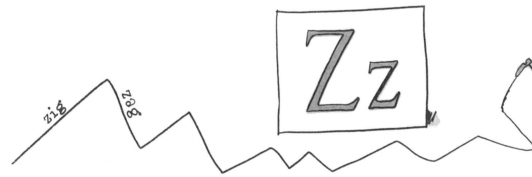

zig
zag

Lowly walked zigzag.

"Very good!" said Miss Honey. "Now, let us all recite our ABC's! Begin!"

`ABCD... EFG... HIJK... LMN... O. P. QRS... TUV... W... X..Y..Z

Now I've said my ABC's;
tell me what you think of me"

17

MAKING THINGS

Miss Honey showed us how to make all kinds of
exciting things with a few simple materials and tools.

embroidery

needle

yarn

weaving

Kathy embroidered with a needle and yarn.

Penny is a weaver.
She wove a table mat.

paste

magazine

scrapbook

crayon

coloring book

Huckle cut pictures out of old
magazines and made a scrapbook.

Charlie colored a coloring
book with crayons.

knitting nancy

Frances knit a sweater for Lowly.

a sweater!

stringing beads

Ruth strung beads on a string.

modeling clay

Willy modeled a bunny
with modeling clay.

Robert built a tower
with building blocks.
Stop, Robert!
That is enough!

building
blocks

making things with paper

paper airplanes

Mary cut out pieces of
paper and folded them.
She made a doll house.

Arthur folded paper, too. He made
paper airplanes. ARTHUR PIG! You know
better than to throw things in class!

19

RECESS ON THE PLAYGROUND

Every day the children have recess. Recess is a time for play.
When the weather is nice they play in the schoolyard.

swing

rings

sliding pole

climbing ladder

hurt knee

shovel

pail

sand box

barrel

hide and seek

ring-a-round-a-rosie

kicking a ball

marbles

jacks

20

see saw

slide

ring toss

tag

leap frog

catching a ball

jump rope

pat-a-cake

hop scotch

stilts

21

THE DAYS OF THE WEEK

At school, Miss Honey teaches us many things.
When she is not teaching, she is very busy doing other things.

On Sunday afternoon she drove out into the country with her friend
Mr. Bruno to have a picnic. Picnics are always fun. Don't you think so?

On Monday after school she did her laundry.

On Tuesday morning before
school, she baked a cake for the
sick children in the hospital.
Mother Cat took it to them.

On Wednesday she made up packages of used clothing to send to children who do not have enough to wear.

On Thursday she met with the principal and the other teachers to plan a school picnic.

On Friday she went to the library to read books and study.
She is always learning new things to teach her children.

On Saturday she did her marketing. And on Saturday night she invited Mr. Bruno for supper. He always brings flowers when he visits. After supper he took Miss Honey to the movies.

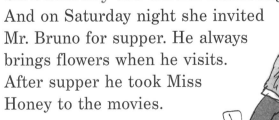

You are a very busy lady, Miss Honey!

LEARNING TO COUNT

0 1 2 3 4 5
zero none one two three four five

6 7 8 9 10
six seven eight nine ten

"Now we shall learn how to count," said Miss Honey.
"Huckle will hold the card showing the correct answer.
How many children are sitting on the stool?" she asked.
The answer is **NONE**. There is no one sitting there.
We use the figure **ZERO** to show **NONE**.

How many flowers are in
the vase on Miss Honey's desk?
You are right, Huckle.
There is just **ONE** flower.

When those little girls
stop talking, how many quiet
girls will there be?
There will be **TWO** quiet girls
when they stop talking.

Roger Raccoon drew a picture of the teacher,
a picture of Huckle, and a picture of Lowly.
If you say he drew **THREE** pictures, you are right!

Arthur Pig had some big marbles
in his pocket. His pocket ripped open
and they fell out.
One, two, three, **FOUR**.
FOUR bouncing marbles.

Miss Honey asked Willy Fox to take the wastebaskets out and empty them. But, Willy, don't take
them all at once! Empty the **FIVE** wastebaskets one at a time! One, two, three, four, **FIVE**.

25

Well! What a mess Willy made! How many brooms did the class use to clean it up?
SIX brooms is the right answer.

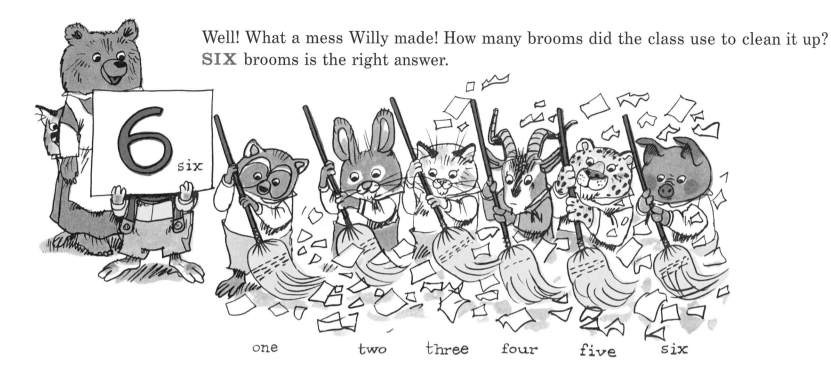

one   two   three   four   five   six

Now, why are all those children raising their hands? It's because they want to ask Miss Honey
for permission to go to the bathroom. You always have to ask, you know. "All right, you may go.
But hurry back," said the teacher. **SEVEN** children left the room to go to the bathroom.

one   two   three   four   five   six   seven

Miss Honey asked Oliver to wipe the chalk off the blackboard with the erasers.
How many erasers did he use? He has **EIGHT** arms so he used **EIGHT** erasers.

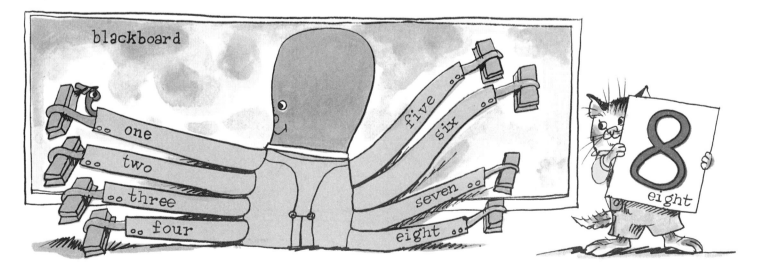

26

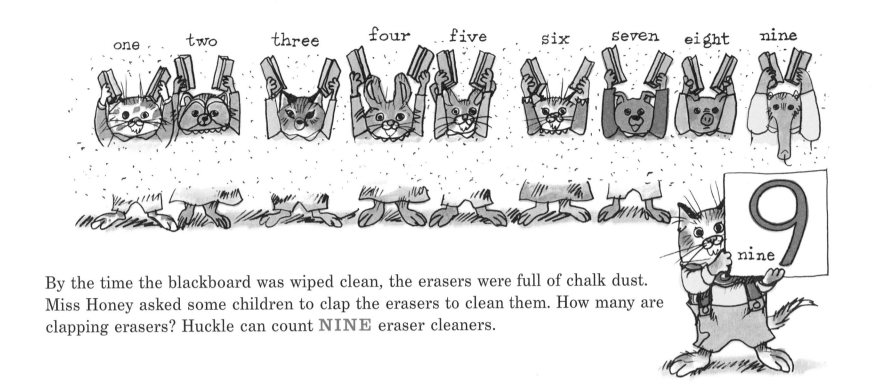

one two three four five six seven eight nine

nine

By the time the blackboard was wiped clean, the erasers were full of chalk dust. Miss Honey asked some children to clap the erasers to clean them. How many are clapping erasers? Huckle can count **NINE** eraser cleaners.

Miss Honey asked Bananas Gorilla what he brought to school to eat at snack time. Did he bring **TEN** bananas? NO! He brought **TEN** bunches of bananas!

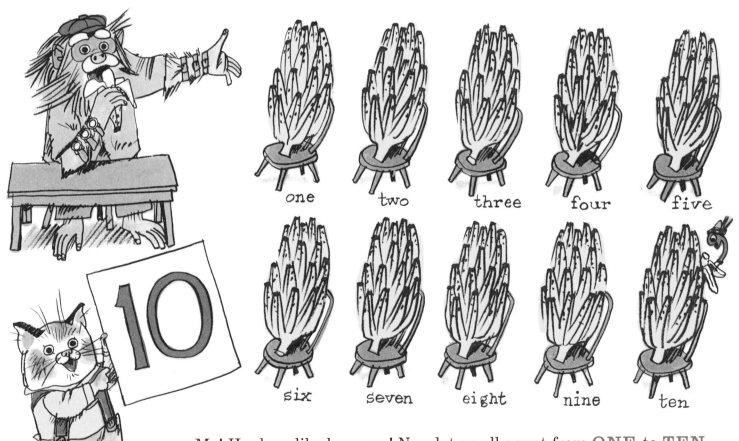

one two three four five

six seven eight nine ten

My! He does like bananas! Now let us all count from **ONE** to **TEN**. One, two, three, four, five, six, seven, eight, nine, ten. Very good, children!

THE HOURS OF THE DAY

It was Saturday. There was no school.
But there were lots of things for Huckle to do.
His friend Lowly was coming to visit for the day.
He was going to stay overnight, too.

At **7 o'clock** Huckle bounced out of bed.

At **8 o'clock** he ate his breakfast.
Father Cat took the tablecloth to work with him again.

At **9 o'clock** he straightened out his room.

At **10 o'clock** he went shopping for food.

At **11 o'clock** he played in his muddy yard with Lowly. He fell down a few times.

12 o'clock is noontime. Huckle and Lowly ate their lunches. Lowly remembered to take his hat off at the table.

At **1 o'clock** they both lay down and had a nap.

At **2 o'clock** they went for a ride. They bumped into Joe, the school janitor. He was on his way to school and he was late again.

At **3 o'clock** they walked home.

At **4 o'clock** they watched television.

At **5 o'clock** Father Cat came home.

At **6 o'clock** Mother Cat served a surprise for supper.
She served Huckle's guest first.

At **7 o'clock** Father Cat gave
Huckle and Lowly their baths.
"Where did that soap go?"
asked Father Cat.

At **8 o'clock** Father Cat read
them a bedtime story in bed.

And at **9 o'clock** they
were sound asleep.
Sleep tight, Huckle!
Sleep tight, Lowly!

MISS HONEY'S BUSY HELPERS

Everyone helps in little ways to
make Miss Honey's life happier.
Miss Honey will never forget the
day when Lowly polished her apple.

That same day
Roger opened
the window and the
papers blew away.

Arthur closed the door
so they wouldn't escape.

Miss Honey remembers that Huckle
sharpened the pencils that day.
He made them a little too short.

Patsy picked papers up off the floor
and put them in the wastebasket.

Eddie erased
the blackboard.

Peter washed the
blackboard with a sponge.

Bobby clapped the erasers.
Miss Honey was about to tell him
to clean them outside when...

...she saw that someone
was watering her plant!

"STOP IT!" she cried.

Why, it was another of her busy helpers!
Joe, the janitor! He had been washing
the outside of her windows.

"Did I get you a little wet?" he asked.
"You forgot to tell someone to close the window!"

OH, JOE!

You should have looked!

35

MEASURING THINGS

"Now we shall learn something about how to measure things," said Miss Honey.

I use a ruler to measure my height.
I am taller than Bugdozer.
He is shorter than I am.

ruler

I use a scale to measure my weight.
I weigh more than Lowly.
He weighs less than I do.
I am heavier than he is.
He is lighter than I am.

scales

My arm is longer than Mouse's.

His arm is shorter than mine.

36

A clock measures time.
I awakened before the sun came up.

Huckle awakened after the sun came up.
I have been awake a longer time than Huckle.
He has been awake a shorter time than I have.

For breakfast I had a hot cup of cocoa.
Huckle had a cold glass of milk.

stove

refrigerator

We make things warm on the stove.
We keep things cool in the refrigerator.

A calendar measures time, too.
It shows the number of days
in the month and the year.

I have had more birthdays than Ruth.
I am older than she is.
Ruth is younger than I am.

My birthday cake has more candles than Ruth's.
Hers has fewer candles than mine.
I have a harder time blowing out the candles
than Ruth does. Ruth has an easier time.

37

SHARES

"Everything has a shape," said Miss Honey.
"I will show you different kinds of shapes. First, look at my shape.
Mr. Bruno says I have a beautiful shape. Would you say that I was fatter
or thinner than Lowly? Yes! I am a little bit fatter than Lowly."

Lowly has been eating peas.
Peas are round in shape.

A ball is round, too.
But Lowly isn't able to eat that.

An egg is oval-shaped.

A block has a square shape.

The moon is sometimes
crescent-shaped.

Oh, yes! Someone sent me a
Valentine in the shape of a heart.
Can you guess who sent it?

I have asked Huckle
to draw some more
shapes for you to see.

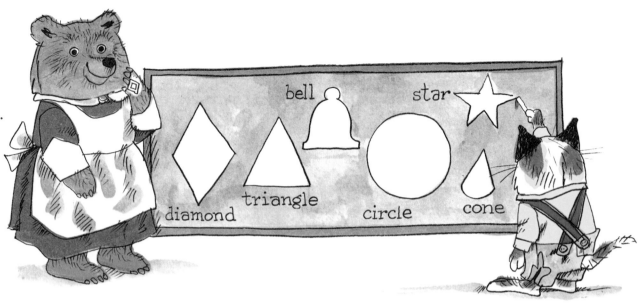

diamond

triangle

bell

circle

star

cone

straight

curved

crooked

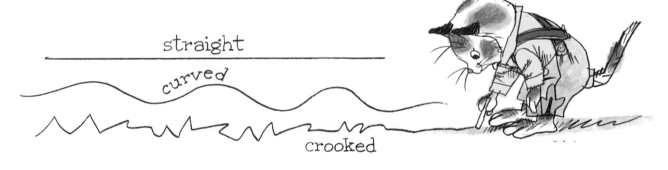

And also some lines.
Thank you, Huckle.

Now, some things change their shape.
A large candle becomes small.

large   small

A short seedling becomes
a tall sunflower.

tiny

great

it's magic!

smoke

fire

wood

And a burning piece of wood turns to smoke and ashes.
Can you think of anything else that changes its shape?
A snowman, maybe? When?

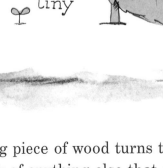

DRAWING AND PAINTING

Drawing and painting are always fun. On drawing and painting days
Miss Honey's class is full of artists. Some artists draw pictures
with crayons or pencils. Some paint pictures with paint and water.
All of them wear smocks so that they won't get their clothes messy.

Huckle helped the teacher pass out
the drawing and painting materials.

These are some of the things he handed to the artists.

pencils

eraser

ball-point pen

pencil sharpener

marker pen

sheets of paper

crayons

paint jars

pastels

water dish

mixing tray

paint brush

paint box

40

At last everyone was ready.

Mildred Hippo placed a pad of paper on her easel. She drew a bug with her pencil.

easel

Elizabeth Rabbit drew a picture with her pastels. She tacked it on the wall.

My Doll

Arthur Pig painted a red apple on the paper.

paint   water

picture

Bobby Cat painted some red footprints on the floor.

Roger Raccoon went to the sink to wash the dirty paint water out of his water dish.
He ran the water too hard.
He made a spatter painting.

sink

My! What a busy group of artists!

41

COLOR

Huckle will show some of the things he has painted.

Red
apple
strawberry
fire engine
heart
the inside of
a watermelon

He painted pictures
of some red things...

Orange
orange
pumpkin
carrot
bus
goldfish

...and some
orange things.

Yellow is a bright sunny color.

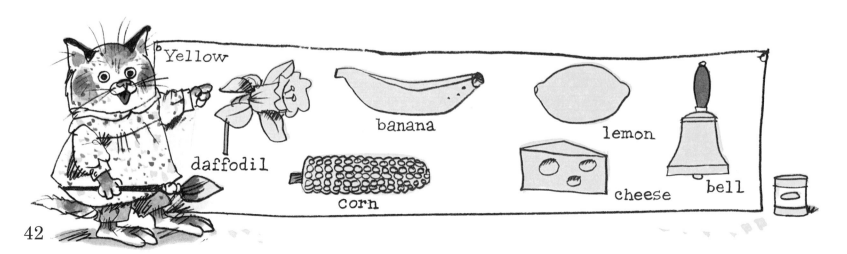

Yellow
daffodil
banana
lemon
corn
cheese
bell

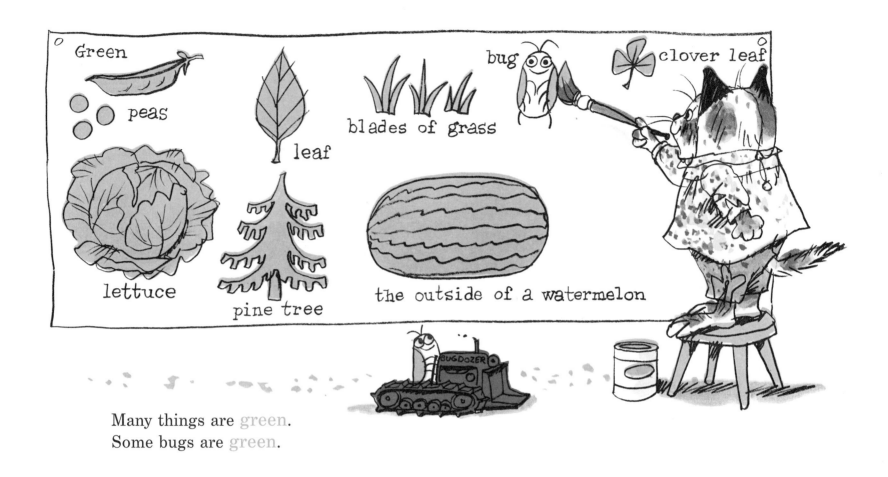

Many things are green.
Some bugs are green.

Huckle painted a blue sky.

When it is cloudy,
the sky is colored gray.
Be careful, Huckle!

43

Huckle painted the floor violet. Purple is almost the same color as violet.

Violet - Purple

violet

pansy

plum

thistle

grapes

Colors can be light or dark. A potato is light brown.
A chocolate Easter bunny is dark brown.

Brown

walnut

shoelace

potato

chocolate
Easter Bunny

light   dark

He painted some black things…   …and some white ones.

Black   doorbell

gumdrop

tire

hat

White

egg

snowman

Besides painting pictures, Huckle painted himself.
Wash the paint off, Huckle, and put on a clean smock. Thank you!

44

MIXING COLORS

Huckle will now show how to mix two colors together to make a third color! Begin, Huckle!

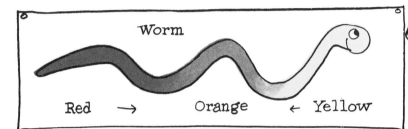

Worm

Red → Orange ← Yellow

Red mixed with yellow makes orange.

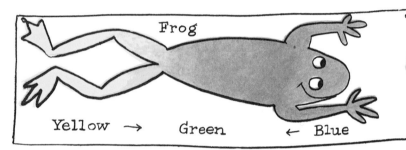

Frog

Yellow → Green ← Blue

Yellow and blue make green.

Lizard

Red → Violet or Purple ← Blue

Red and blue make violet or purple.

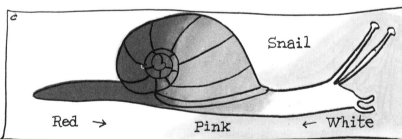

Snail

Red → Pink ← White

Red and white make pink.

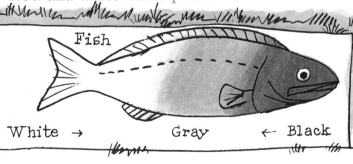

Fish

White → Gray ← Black

White and black make gray.

You are a fine color mixer, Huckle. Now, will YOU be able to remember how to mix colors the next time you paint? Of course, you will!

SHOW AND TELL

One of the best times at school is "Show and Tell" time. Huckle is going to tell about the exciting time he had last summer when he visited his Uncle Willie's farm. Let's listen.

Huckle started to tell his story.
"Well, first of all," he said, "I had to get to my uncle's farm. My mother and father took me to the airport and put me on an airplane.

"I flew to another airport near my uncle's farm. My uncle was waiting for me on the airport runway. We almost landed on top of him!

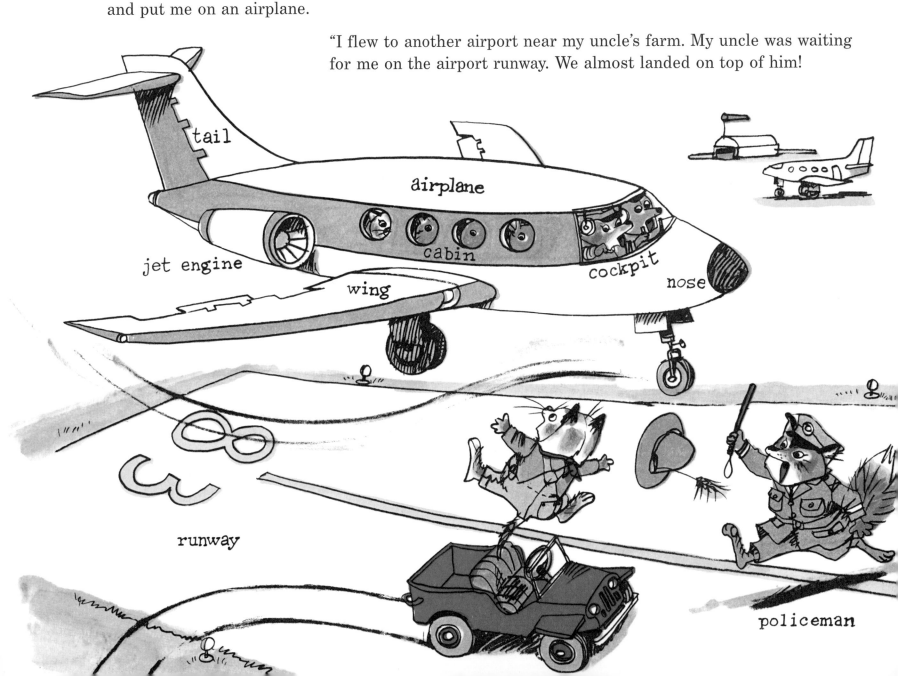

tail

airplane

jet engine

cabin

cockpit

nose

wing

runway

policeman

"We drove to Uncle Willie's farm," said Huckle.
"When we got there, my Aunt Millie
was cooking in the kitchen. She is a good cook.

"Hens and roosters are chickens.
Hens have to eat before they will lay eggs.
I fed them grain and corn. Uncle Willie gathered the eggs.
Roosters don't lay eggs. They crow. Cock-a-doodle-doo! Cock-a-doodle-doo!

47

"I fed hay to the cows. Cows make milk. Uncle Willie milked them. We put the cans of milk in the farm truck and drove to the dairy.

"At the dairy many things are done with the milk.
Some milk is put in cartons and sold at the market for drinking.
Some milk is made into butter. Some is made into cheese.
And, best of all, some is made into ice cream. The dairy man gave me an ice cream cone.

48

"Then we went back to the farm
and plowed a field to make it
ready for planting seeds.
Uncle Willie let me steer the tractor!

"Uncle Willie planted all kinds of seeds.
I planted one pumpkin seed. It would take
all summer to grow. I hoped it would grow
into a big pumpkin.

"Uncle Willie finished planting.
He asked me to drive to the barn
and get the wagon.
He wanted to pick his vegetables
and take them to market.

49

"We filled the wagon with vegetables from Uncle Willie's garden.
Uncle Willie sat on top of them so that none would fall off.
Then we drove to the farmers' market.

spinach

cabbage

potatoes

cauliflower

turnip

asparagus

beans

"At the market I parked right next
to a water hydrant," said Huckle.
"I delivered the vegetables to
Uncle Willie's vegetable stand.

PUMPKIN

50

celery

tomatoes

lettuce

corn

beets

squash

peas

UNCLE WILLIE'S VEGETABLES

carrots

onions

FARMERS' MARKET
FRUIT STAND

plums   blueberries   cherries   pears   grapes   banana

raspberries   tangerines   apples   oranges   peaches

pineapple   strawberries   lemons   grapefruit   watermelon

51

"Well! That was the end of my summer vacation," said Huckle.
"I was sent back home. Uncle Willie promised to bring my pumpkin
to me when it was fully grown.

"And he did!
And now I am going to show it to you!
I am also going to show you
what I made with it!"

Why, Huckle! That just has to be the BIGGEST jack-o-lantern ever!
You are not only a good pumpkin grower, you are also a good jack-o-lantern maker!
Isn't he, children? But be careful that you don't frighten that witch with it!

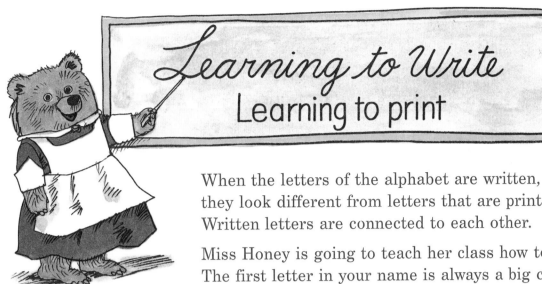

Learning to Write
Learning to print

When the letters of the alphabet are written,
they look different from letters that are printed.
Written letters are connected to each other.

Miss Honey is going to teach her class how to write.
The first letter in your name is always a big capital letter.
The others are small letters.

This is how Albert's name looks printed: Albert

And this is how it looks written: *Albert*

A a
A a

Albert has an apple in his hand
Albert has an apple in his hand

B b
B b

Bananas Gorilla is being silly
Bananas Gorilla is being silly

C c
C c

Charlie Anteater is chewing gum
Charlie Anteater is chewing gum

That is very nice writing, boys!

"Now, Huckle," said Miss Honey, "will you please write all the letters of the alphabet? I want all the children to copy them. With a little help, maybe they will be able to write their own names."

sharpen your pencil!

Aa Bb Cc Dd

Aa Bb Cc Dd

Ee Ff Gg Hh

Ee Ff Gg Hh

Ii Jj Kk Ll

Ii Jj Kk Ll

Mm Nn Oo Pp

Mm Nn Oo Pp

Qq Rr Ss Tt

Qq Rr Ss Tt

Uu Vv Ww Xx

Uu Vv Ww Xx

Yy Zz

Yy Zz

Now, everyone, please take a pencil and a paper and try to write your own name.

VISITING THE DOCTOR'S OFFICE

From time to time all the children must visit the doctor. He examines them to make sure that they are well and healthy. This was the day for Doctor Bear to look at them and make them say AHHHH. All right! Everyone get in line and file into the doctor's office. Take off your shirts and blouses.

Nurse Nelly measured the children to see how tall they were growing.
She weighed them to see how heavy they were.

height measure

scales

Doctor Bear made everyone say AHHHH.
He looked inside their throats. He held his stethoscope against their bare chests and listened. It tickled.

Doctor Bear said that everyone was well and healthy.

bandages

scissors

thermometer

flashlight

tongue
stick

adhesive tape

The doctor comes to visit the school only on certain days.
But Nurse Nelly is at school every day.
She looks after any child who isn't feeling well.

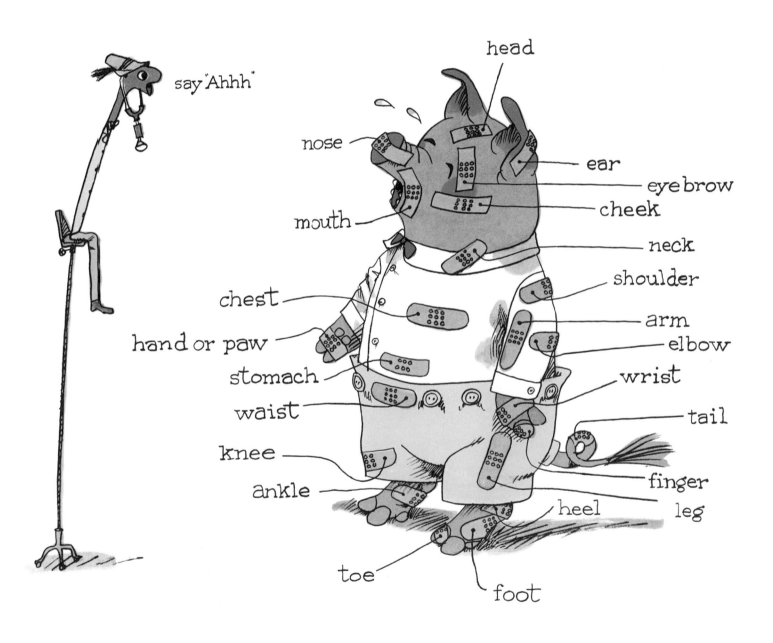

say "Ahhh"

head
nose
ear
eyebrow
cheek
mouth
neck
shoulder
chest
arm
hand or paw
elbow
stomach
wrist
waist
tail
knee
ankle
finger
leg
heel
toe
foot

Arthur Pig fell down and hurt himself in the schoolyard.
"Where does it hurt?" Nurse Nelly asked Arthur.
"Everywhere!" said Arthur.
So Nurse Nelly put bandages everywhere to make him stop hurting.

57

JANITOR JOE
AND THE MONTHS OF THE YEAR

Joe is our school janitor.
A janitor takes care of the schoolhouse.
He fixes things when they get broken.
He works around the school
all twelve months of the year.

The first month of the year is January. January is a snowy month.
When it snows, Joe shovels a path through the deep snow.

In February he spreads sand
on the icy sidewalk so that no one will slip.

What happened?
Did you slip, Joe?

In March the strong winds blow.
Joe empties the wastebaskets into the trash burner outside.

The Easter Bunny comes in April

In April the rain falls from the sky and makes the
plants grow. Joe makes sure that the plants growing
in the school flower garden get plenty of water.

In May Joe mows the school lawn with this lawnmower.
Once the mower got away and ran into a supermarket.
Do you suppose it was tired of chewing on nothing but grass?

In June Miss Honey asked Joe to fix a table.
One leg wobbled a little bit.

Well he really fixed that table, didn't he?
You can fix it correctly during
our summer vacation.
We will see you in the fall.
Keep the school looking nice, Joe!

In July, when everyone was away on vacation,
Joe gave everything a fresh coat of paint.

61

The month of August is very hot and sunny.
That's when Joe fixed the showers in the gym.
He pretended that he was at the seashore.

In September school begins again. Joe made a new cement sidewalk for the
children to walk on. It is now soft and wet. Tomorrow it will be hard and dry.
I think you should have made it a few days sooner, Joe!

nice work, Joe!

I love the smell of burning leaves!

In October, the leaves begin to fall.
Joe raked them up and carried them
in his wheelbarrow to a big pile.
He burned them in an open place
so nothing else would catch fire.

JOE! You left the wheelbarrow too close to the fire!

November is a cold and windy month.
Winter is coming. Joe sawed the dead branches off
the trees so they wouldn't be broken off by the wind
and fall on top of something. The principal came out to look at his new car.

63

In December there are lots of holiday celebrations. Joe put up the school Christmas tree. He decorated it with ornaments. It looks beautiful.

To complete his work, Joe has only to put the star on the top of the tree.

Can you reach it, Joe?

THE SCHOOL LIBRARY

Now, where was Miss Honey taking the children?
She was taking them to the school library!
She was going to read stories to them out of some
of the library books.

The library shelves were full of all kinds of books.
Miss Honey gathered her children around her and read some exciting stories.

She read a fairy tale about a pretty princess and a brave knight.
The knight had a fight with a dragon.

She told them a story about a little Inuit boy who
lived in an igloo far away in the cold North.
An igloo is a house made of blocks and ice.

"Look at the picture of the Inuit boy paddling
his kayak in the water," said Miss Honey.

When she finished reading Miss Honey said, "Any child who can write his name on a library card will be able to take a book home to read."

Miss Honey took a rubber stamp and stamped a date in Huckle's book. Now he will know on what day he must return the book to the library. The other children waited their turn to borrow a book.

Huckle rode home on the school bus.

Mother Cat was waiting for him.

Huckle showed her his library card.
She was so pleased to find that Huckle could write his own name!
"Huckle! You are really learning a lot in school!" she said.
Huckle hurried into the house to read his book.

67

Now, at least once every school year, Miss Honey takes the children on a school picnic.
Mr. Bruno was invited, too. He cooked the hot dogs.
Miss Honey poured the lemonade. Bananas Gorilla played his Banana Guitar.
Huckle scooped out the ice cream. Joe brought his kite and showed everyone how to fly it.
Lowly won the Sack Race.

And a very good time was had by one and all!

68

FINISH LINE